Paddington's
GUIDE TO
LONDON

A BEAR'S EYE VIEW

PADDINGTON'S
MAP OF CENTRAL
LONDON

PHOTO CREDITS:

Front cover (Big Ben) and pages 17 (bottom), 60, 65, 73 (left), 81, 83 (left), 93 (both),
97 (bottom), 105 © / used under licence from Shutterstock. Page 12 © Holmes Garden Photos /
Alamy, page 22(top) © Travelshots.com / Alamy, page 23 © Robert Estall photo agency / Alamy.
Page 104 courtesy of Jason's Trip. Pages 28 (background), 30 (background), 41 (background),
43 (background), 51 (background), 98, 99 (background), 101 (background) copyright ©
HarperCollins*Publishers* Ltd 2011

Composite photographs on pages 5, 8, 10, 14, 16, 17 (top), 19, 20, 24, 27, 90, 92,
94, 97 (top), 102, 110, 111, 112, 114, 123: background images © / used under licence
from Shutterstock; inside front cover and page 109 (ice cream), page 41 (chips) © / used under
licence from Shutterstock. Page 13 background image © Londonstills.com / Alamy.
All images of Paddington Bear by Laura Ashman copyright
© HarperCollins*Publishers* Ltd 2011

Additional photographs by Laura Ashman, copyright © HarperCollins*Publishers* Ltd 2011

First published in paperback in the United Kingdom by
HarperCollins *Children's Books* in 2011
This edition published in 2022

HarperCollins *Children's Books* is a division of HarperCollins*Publishers* Ltd
1 London Bridge Street, London, SE1 9GF

www.harpercollins.co.uk

HarperCollins*Publishers*
1st Floor, Watermarque Building, Ringsend Road, Dublin 4, Ireland

1 3 5 7 9 10 8 6 4 2

Text copyright © Michael Bond 2011, 2016, 2022
Maps copyright © HarperCollins*Publishers* Ltd 2011, 2022

ISBN: 978-0-00-849966-2

Printed in Bosnia and Herzegovina

Paddington's GUIDE TO LONDON

A BEAR'S EYE VIEW

Michael Bond

HarperCollins *Children's Books*

CONTENTS

INTRODUCTION

According to my best friend, Mr Gruber, in the old days a great deal of London was made up of separate villages (as was the case with many other capital cities of the world). In 1773 no fewer than forty-six were listed, and Paddington was one of them. Over the years, as they grew larger and prospered, they eventually merged with each other and became part of one enormous whole.

Mr Gruber keeps an antique shop in the Portobello Road, and although he wasn't around at the time, he knows about these things.

He says that while the inhabitants of these villages could hardly prevent it happening, they steadfastly refused to change their way of life, and we should be grateful they stood their ground, for it is one of the reasons why London is such a diverse city.

Since I arrived in England Mr Gruber has taken me on lots of outings and I can see what he means. For example, the people who live in Fitzrovia are very different from those in Stoke Newington, and both are different again to the ones who live in the Elephant and Castle, on the other side of the River Thames, where I have yet to see a castle, let alone an elephant.

A famous man called Dr Johnson once said, "When a man is tired of London, he is tired of life". That was in 1777, so there is even more to see nowadays.

Dr Johnson isn't the only one who was good at thinking up quotations. I once had a letter from a small boy in America who said he was so used to Paddington being the name of a bear, it now seemed a funny name for a railway station.

I know just what he meant. When I first set foot on Paddington Station there were so many people rushing to and fro I didn't know which way to go, so I sat on my suitcase outside the lost property office and waited for something to happen, which it did, of course.

I was befriended by a lovely family called the Browns, who took me home to live with them and their two children, Jonathan and Judy, not to mention their housekeeper, Mrs Bird. But that's another story.

My Aunt Lucy, who lives in the Home for Retired Bears in Lima, says you should always begin at the beginning, so that is why I'm starting with Paddington.

"Hello, everybody!"

PADDINGTON
STATION

It's hard to picture Paddington Station ever having been part of a small village. Mr Gruber told me that there was a time when it only had one letter "d" in its name. I said, "Perhaps they couldn't spell very well in those days, Mr Gruber," and he replied, "Some things never change, Mr Brown."

Nowadays Paddington is so busy that up to 80,000 people pass through the station every day. On Platform Eight there is a statue in memory of Isambard Kingdom Brunel. He was the son of a French engineer and he not only designed the station, but was responsible for the whole of what was then called the Great Western Railway –

building bridges and viaducts, digging tunnels and laying the tracks, so I expect that's why he's sitting down. He must have been tired after all the hard work.

I didn't dream that one day I would also have a statue on the station. It's on a marble plinth alongside Platform One. During the summer people join me to eat their sandwiches while they wait for a train, but in the winter the marble gets very cold, so they don't sit on it quite so much! I often wonder what Mr Brunel would make of it all if he could see them. Mr Gruber thinks he might say, "*Nom d'un nom!*" – which is French for "Whatever is the world coming to?"

"This is me!"

As well as my statue there is a shop and even a café dedicated to me, which is definitely worth a visit if you fancy trying a marmalade sandwich or a cup of Peruvian coffee.

If you want to explore the area there are lots of free guided walks, including several especially meant for children. However, if you leave the station from the exit near my statue, and climb up some steps into Eastbourne Terrace, then turn left and follow it through until it becomes Spring Street, you will find it is only a short walk to Hyde Park and one of the first places in London I ever visited. You can't miss it because it's over a mile and a half long and the Bayswater Road runs alongside it all the way.

HYDE PARK

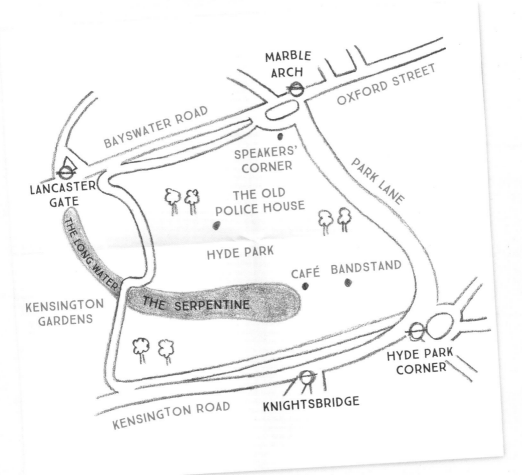

Once upon a time Hyde Park was one of several parks belonging to King Henry VIII and he used it to hunt deer and wild boar. But in the early seventeenth century King Charles I opened its 350 acres of woods and grassland to the public, and although it is still a Royal Park, it is now a playground for anybody who likes to go there. As you might imagine, after a long sea voyage stowed away in a lifeboat it felt like a dream come true to me.

In the middle, in the Old Police House, there is an enquiry booth, but the following are a few ideas to be going on with.

First of all, there is a huge artificial lake that was made by damming the Westbourne River. Because of its shape it's called the Serpentine, and if you don't mind sharing it with ducks and swans, you can swim in a part of it called the Lido. There is a café nearby, and a paddling pool for small children.

Hyde Park

"It's like being at the seaside"

↖ The Serpentine

On the main part of the lake there are over 100 rowing boats and pedalos for hire, or you can simply cross from one side to the other on the SolarShuttle which has room for up to forty passengers and gets its power from solar panels embedded in the roof.

You need to buy tickets for all these things, of course, including the use of deckchairs… but everything else in the park is free. There are acres of grass to play on, benches for watching the world go by, occasional concerts in the bandstand on Sundays, a "playground" for the elderly, and sometimes, when it's the Queen's birthday or some other royal anniversary, you can watch the King's Troop Royal Horse Artillery arrive to fire a 41-gun royal salute. That's twenty more than a normal 21-gun royal salute. The extra twenty are because of it being a Royal Park.

It's very exciting seeing them arrive. I wouldn't mind being a trooper, but Mrs Bird says I wouldn't be allowed to wear my duffle coat and I might fall off my horse at the wrong moment.

Another free piece of entertainment takes place every Sunday morning in the northeast corner of the park. It's in an area known as Speakers' Corner.

Since 1872, anyone armed with a box to stand on can address the assembled crowds on whatever subject they feel strongly about, without fear of being arrested.

When I went with Mr Gruber he asked me what I would choose if I had a box.

I said straight away, "I'm glad you asked me that, Mr Gruber. Things that are shrink-wrapped in plastic. I don't think manufacturers ever give a thought to what it must be like if you are a bear. I bought a card for my Aunt Lucy the other week and it took me all the morning to find a way in. I had to borrow Mr Brown's tool box and it ended up saying "APPY BIRTHDA". But it did save on postage.

"That's another thing. The cost of posting letters to Peru is going up all the time… I would like to do something about that too…"

People were cheering me on by then and one man said he thought they ought to make me Prime Minister.

Mr Gruber beat what he called "a hasty retreat" to Kensington Gardens, which is attached to the western edge of Hyde Park. It's so well done I couldn't see the join no matter how hard I looked.

Speakers' Corner

"Is anyone going to Peru?"

KENSINGTON GARDENS

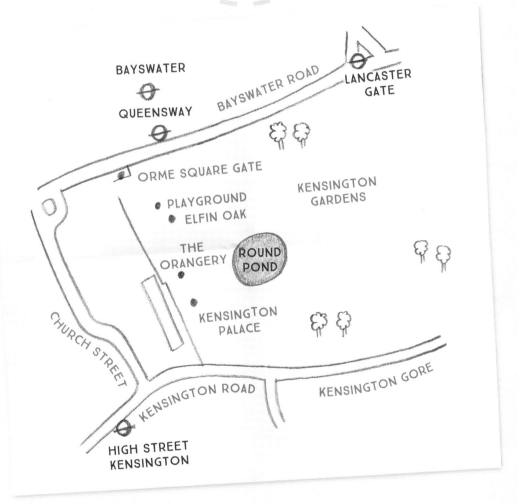

Round Pond ↘

"This is a picture of me having my elevenses"

The first thing you pass as you head towards Kensington Palace from Hyde Park is the Round Pond. It's hard to miss because it covers an area of seven acres and is very popular with children sailing their boats.

There is a restaurant called the Orangery in the Palace grounds, but it was too early for lunch, so while Mr Gruber paid a quick visit to the Palace to see if there was anything new, I had my elevenses.

Afterwards he took me to see Princess Diana's adventure playground that not only has swings and slides, but there is a huge model pirate ship that seemed very popular. We didn't go in because it's for children only and bears weren't mentioned, but Mr Gruber showed me a giant tree stump called the Elfin Oak because of all the tiny elves carved on it.

We left Kensington Gardens by the Orme Square Gate, turned left into the Bayswater Road, and having made our way past the vast Russian Consulate – at which point the Bayswater Road becomes Notting Hill Gate – found ourselves in Notting Hill.

Elfin Oak

NOTTING
HILL

Notting Hill Gate used to be part of an old Roman road leading to Silchester, and one theory is that its inhabitants were called "sons of Cnotta". The "gate" was a spiked barrier to stop invaders. In the 1800s it was the haunt of highwaymen, but nowadays it has two cinemas, the Coronet and the Gate. The Coronet has half-price seats all day on Tuesdays, and afterwards you can find plenty of restaurants to choose from around the corner on Hillgate Street.

If you carry straight on down Holland Park Avenue and turn left by a statue labelled St Volodymyr, Ruler of Ukraine 980–1015, a little way up the hill, you will find yourself outside the entrance to the Holland Park wildlife reserve.

Entry is free and the park is open from dawn to dusk. That end of it is full of wildlife. Rabbits, squirrels and pheasants take cover when they see you coming, but further in peacocks hardly give you a second glance. They are too busy preening themselves.

Japanese Kyoto Garden

"London is full of surprises"

There is an adventure playground for older children and another with sandpits for the tiny tots. Further in still, there is a formal Japanese Kyoto Garden with waterfalls and bridges.

There is also a picnic area, an ecology centre and the Holland Park Café, along with tennis courts and an open-air theatre.

SHEPHERD'S BUSH

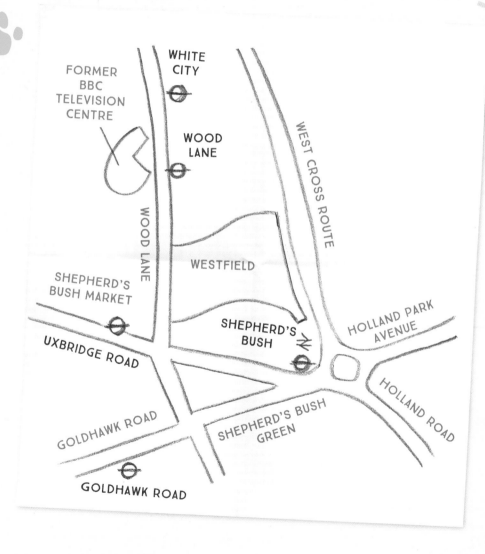

FORMER BBC TELEVISION CENTRE

WHITE CITY

WOOD LANE

WEST CROSS ROUTE

WOOD LANE

WESTFIELD

SHEPHERD'S BUSH MARKET

SHEPHERD'S BUSH

HOLLAND PARK AVENUE

UXBRIDGE ROAD

HOLLAND ROAD

GOLDHAWK ROAD

SHEPHERD'S BUSH GREEN

GOLDHAWK ROAD

If you have spent the morning in Hyde Park and none of these things happens to appeal to you, then carry on down Holland Park Avenue to Shepherd's Bush where the former BBC Television Centre, once the biggest landmark in the area, is now dwarfed by Westfield – Europe's largest indoor shopping mall.

Despite being the size of thirty football pitches rolled into one, Westfield is said to be very family friendly. I expect it is if you are a footballer and know where the goalposts are likely to be, but I think I would soon get lost. Inside, there are branches of practically all the big names in the world of high street shopping; a multiplex cinema complex; a Playworld for the under-fives; also over fifty places to eat.

Some people stay there all day, but Mr Gruber thinks it might not appeal to everybody.

Depending on the time it would be a good idea to take a taxi, bus or the Underground train and head east, towards Notting Hill Gate where, if it's a nice day, there's a very pleasant walk up Holland Park Avenue.

However, if instead of heading west down Holland Park Avenue, you had decided to go north up Pembridge Road, then you should take the second turning to the left into the Portobello Road.

PORTOBELLO ROAD

LADBROKE GROVE

PORTOBELLO ROAD

WESTWAY

GREAT WESTERN ROAD

WESTBOURNE PARK

LANCASTER ROAD

PARK ROAD

LADBROKE GROVE

WESTBOURNE

CHEPSTOW ROAD

BLENHEIM CRES.

COLVILLE TERRACE

ELGIN CRES.

MUSEUM OF BRANDS, PACKAGING & ADVERTISING

PORTOBELLO ROAD

LADBROKE GROVE

KENSINGTON PARK ROAD

PEMBRIDGE ROAD

NOTTING HILL

NOTTING HILL GATE

HOLLAND PARK AVENUE

NOTTING HILL GATE

Portobello Road is home to one of the largest street markets in the world; one mile long, it began life in 1870. As you make your way down the hill more and more antique shops come into view, until eventually they occupy both sides of the road, selling not only furniture and silverware, but everything from inn signs to ancient typewriters, old clocks, postcards, musical instruments, locks, door knockers – the list is endless.

Gradually, antique shops give way to fruit and vegetable stalls, and beyond that there is a clothes market with everything from 1920s clothing to up-and-coming young designers displaying the latest in fashion accessories. The famous men's tailor, Ozwald Boateng, began his career with a stall there.

Portobello Road

Portobello Road

"I don't think the man liked me squeezing his oranges"

Blenheim Crescent

Nowadays the whole area is full of interesting shops. Before you reach the clothes market, if you turn left into Blenheim Crescent, there is Books for Cooks, where they stock everything written about food you can possibly think of. The nice smell that greets you when you go inside is because they serve lunch in a tiny area at the back of the shop. I don't suppose they ever run out of new recipes to try!

Across the road there is a travel bookshop that was the inspiration for the film *Notting Hill*, with Julia Roberts and Hugh Grant. (So many people paid a visit after the film came out, the owners had to paint their front door a different colour!)

While you are exploring the area, watch out for a baker's. It could be where I buy my buns. On sunny days, Mr Gruber and I often have our elevenses sitting in deckchairs outside his shop. But that's only at the beginning of the week. By the time Saturday comes round, the road is closed to traffic. Overnight hundreds of extra traders have set up their stalls, and the pavements are alive with sightseers and street entertainers.

When that happens we take shelter on an old horsehair sofa at the back of his shop and discuss things in general.

"I'm glad Mr Gruber's shop isn't as crammed with things as this one. We wouldn't have room for our 'elevenses'"

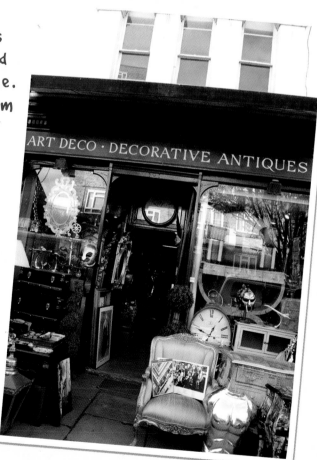

MARYLEBONE

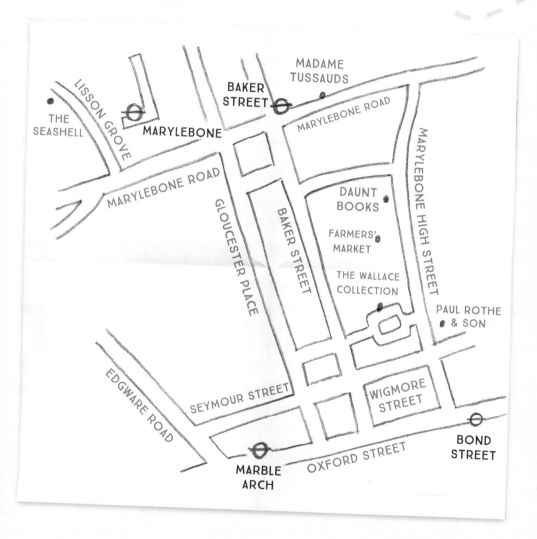

It was a Saturday morning when Mr Gruber told me about Marylebone, which in the beginning was also a small village, twinned with Paddington.

Marylebone has a railway station too, but because it was one of the last to be built in London it only had two platforms, and the trains never really went anywhere exciting. Even when more platforms were added, it spent a lot of its life pretending to be somewhere else, when film and television makers weren't allowed to use the real thing.

It stood in for Paddington Station when The Beatles made *A Hard Day's Night*, and again in *The Ipcress File* with Michael Caine. Agatha Christie's *4.50 from Paddington* was filmed there. Then it became Waterloo Station for the BBC, when an updated Reginald Perrin series was being made for television.

"Now you see them;
now you don't!"

I think it must be very confusing for anyone travelling. They probably don't know whether they are catching the 4.30 train to Aylesbury or taking part in a film.

It makes me realise how lucky I was to end up being called Paddington. Apart from everything else, it sounds more down to earth.

Having said that, Marylebone isn't too grand to have what Mr Gruber calls "the other" best fish and chip shop in London: the Seashell of Lisson Grove – which is only a short walk from the station. In the evening lots of taxi cabs are parked nearby. He says that is always a good sign.

Madame Tussauds

The station has also drawn what Mr Gruber calls "the short straw" when it comes to anyone visiting Marylebone's most famous attraction: Madame Tussauds. Baker Street Underground station beats it by several train lengths. But if you go out into the main Marylebone Road and follow the line of traffic you can see the queues in the distance, so there is no need to ask the way.

Although it is possible to get fast-track entry tickets to Madame Tussauds in advance, most people seem perfectly happy to wait for hours in all weathers to see wax models of famous people down through history, as have many millions of others before them since it first opened in 1884.

I'm glad my statue was modelled in bronze. Had it been wax, my whiskers might have dropped off by now with the heat from all the crowds.

It must be even worse if you are an attendant. Sometimes they stand very still for minutes on end, pretending they are made of wax. Small boys come along and stamp on their feet just to see if they are real or not. I expect the attendants would like to put them in their old Chamber of Horrors. I know I would – especially if I wasn't wearing my wellingtons.

Mr Gruber says Marylebone was originally built by an Act of Parliament when it became part of London, which is why many of the streets look exactly the same, so it's all the more surprising the main street still has a village feel to it.

There is a farmers' market in a nearby car park every Sunday, and while the high street might not be very long from beginning to end, it does have everything you might need during the week.

Marylebone Farmers' Market

"Now I wish I'd brought my shopping basket on wheels"

Daunt Book

"There were so many books it was a bit daunting at first"

DAUNT BOOKS

In amongst the many boutiques, fashionable dress shops and cafés there is The Conran Shop for household furnishings and gifts for every occasion, and Daunt Books – one of London's best book shops, where the latest titles are displayed with their jackets facing outwards.

Then there is FishWorks, which not only sells fresh fish, but has a small restaurant at the back with a special children's menu for those who deserve to be rewarded with a fishcake and tomato sauce after all the window-shopping.

Marylebone High Street

Wallace Collection

Near the end of it all, in Manchester Square, stands one of the most child-friendly small museums in London: the Wallace Collection, home to Frans Hals' *The Laughing Cavalier* and a magnificent collection of old armour, weaponry and paintings housed in a grand eighteenth-century town house. Every room is filled with treasures.

Special events are held throughout the year and in the courtyard there is a first-class brasserie, which is open all day for snacks, ice creams and meals.

However, if you fancy quieter surroundings, at 35 Marylebone Lane there is a delicatessen owned by Paul Rothe & Son. They not only serve meat and vegetable soups, but they specialise in making the best sandwiches ever from ingredients of your choice, to be eaten on the premises amid shelves packed with old-fashioned jams and chutneys, or to take away.

Mr Gruber says that although the Rothe family have been making sandwiches for over one hundred years, the bread is absolutely fresh and he can't think of a better way to prepare yourself for the rigours of Oxford Street, if that's where you plan to go next.

"The bag is what is known as 'temporary accommodation'!"

OXFORD STREET

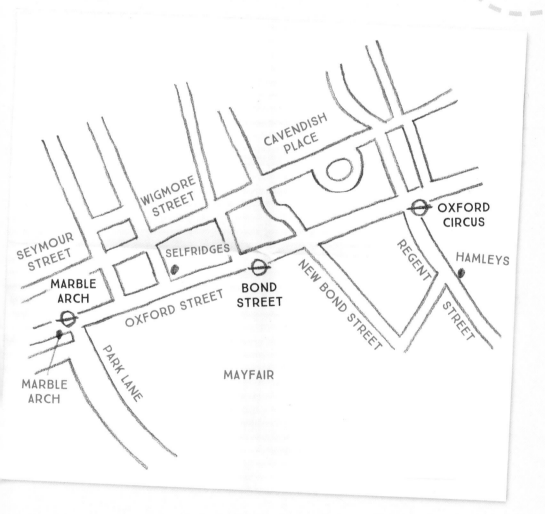

The first time I went to Oxford Street it was on a shopping expedition to buy a duffle coat, and I remember thinking what a funny idea it was – naming a street after another city. It wouldn't be a good start to anybody's day if they walked the quarter mile or so to Marble Arch and found they still had another forty miles to go.

Then I discovered that it had once been called Tyburn Road, which led on past Marble Arch into what is now the Bayswater Road, and some gallows where there were public hangings. I can see why they might want to change the names of the streets.

If they had asked me, I would have called it "Selfridge Street", because it is home to one of the biggest department stores in the country. Selfridges has been there since 1909 and is famous for its window displays.

Marble Arch

Selfridges

The year it opened they had the plane in which Louis Blériot had just made the first solo flight across the English Channel, and in 1925 John Logie Baird gave the first public demonstration of British television. I expect it was a cookery programme, even in those days.

I say that because I once went into a shop window by mistake and a display of saucepans rained down on me. A large crowd collected at the time.

On the other hand, Oxford Street is full of large stores: John Lewis, Marks & Spencer and many others. They act like a magnet to the crowds, and all of them would probably like the street to be named after them, but as Mr Gruber says, "You can't please all the people all the time."

He is right, of course, but there are exceptions to every rule.

New Bond Street

Halfway along Oxford Street, past a turning into New Bond Street which is full of jewellers' shops (I tried doing my Christmas shopping there one year and not one of them had anything for sixpence!) you come to a big road junction called Oxford Circus. You can't miss it because it's the only one in London where the pedestrian crossings go diagonally as well as straight across, which is very confusing. So watch out – you might meet yourself coming back the other way!

If you turn right and make your way down Regent Street, on the left-hand side of the road there is a store that has managed to please all the children all the time for over 250 years.

Hamleys, one of the largest and most famous toy shops in the world, attracts some five million visitors annually.

All five floors are packed with products and there is something happening whichever way you look. Model planes zoom overhead. Radio-controlled cars follow you around. Stuffed toys cry out for attention. Magicians make things disappear before your very eyes, and model trains come and go along seemingly endless tracks.

Hamleys was bombed five times during World War II, but still managed to survive. Holder of two Royal Warrants, nowadays it has outlets as far apart as Denmark and Dubai.

As we carried on down Regent Street, Mr Gruber said he imagined I must wish there had been a Hamleys near me when I was a cub.

"I wouldn't have had anywhere to keep my things in Darkest Peru, Mr Gruber," I said. "I spent most of my time up a tree. I was very lucky, though. My uncle gave me an old cocoa tin that had a stone inside. Shaking it kept me happy for hours on end."

Mr Gruber said it was food for thought and he would bear it in mind the next time he went shopping for toys.

I think the mention of food set both our minds working, but by then we had reached the bottom of Regent Street.

At which point, when it came to writing this book I wanted to put "for adults only", but Mr Gruber said if I did that it would only make children want to read it all the more, so it was much better to tell the truth…

Hamleys

PICCADILLY

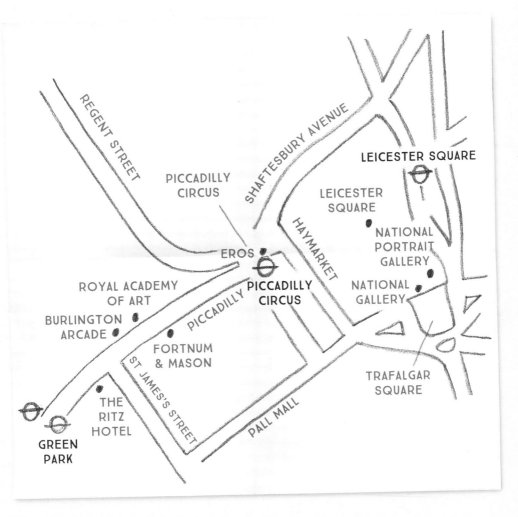

Piccadilly Circus

Well, the truth is that while Piccadilly Circus might be one of the most famous places in the world, apart from all the lights (and Mrs Bird would have something to say about leaving them on all day), after the excitement of Hamleys, the West End of London is a bit of a let-down for small children.

To start with, it isn't a real circus — there are no elephants or tightrope walkers. It is simply a place where lots of well-known streets meet up. Also, again according to Mr Gruber, the statue of a man with a bow and arrow on top of a fountain in the middle of it isn't Eros the god of love, as most people believe, but his twin brother, Anteros. The person who modelled for it was Angelo Colarossi, aged sixteen. I don't suppose he ever realised how famous he became, although not many people would have recognised him with his clothes on.

His arrow used to point up Shaftesbury Avenue, otherwise known as London's Theatreland, but he seems to have lost it. Perhaps it happened the same night as the Browns took me to see my first play.

Mr Brown said we had a box and I pictured the sort of box people use at Speakers' Corner on a Sunday. Imagine my surprise when it turned out to be a small room with one side missing so that you could look down on to the stage. In my excitement I accidentally dropped a marmalade sandwich over the side and it landed on a man's head in the stalls.

Jonathan said he probably wondered what hit him. And Mrs Bird said he would know soon enough when he looked in a mirror. I don't suppose he goes to the theatre very much these days. I don't either.

Another famous street leading off Piccadilly Circus is Piccadilly itself. It was named after a tailor made a fortune selling fancy shirt collars known as "piccadills", and afterwards built a house called Pikadilly Hall on the proceeds.

Shaftesbury Avenue

"I must say, Les looks a bit miserable"

Nowadays it is part of the A4 trunk road entering London, and its worldwide reputation rests on a few shops and a hotel, all on the south side.

First in line is Waterstones, one of the largest book shops in Europe. The other two stores, both holders of Royal Warrants, are Hatchards book shop, which has been there since 1797 and currently holds three warrants, and Fortnum & Mason, purveyors of luxury foods and specialist household items, who have held many such honours over the past 150 years.

They created the Scotch egg in the eighteenth century, and are famous for their luxury hampers for people who are lucky enough to be able to afford them. The staff in the food department still wear tail coats, even if they are only selling you a tin of sardines.

Fortnum & Mason

"I wouldn't mind being an assistant in the marmalade department!"

Fortnum & Mason

There is a large clock high above the front door and when it finishes striking the hour, doors on either side of it open and effigies of Mr Fortnum and Mr Mason slowly emerge against a background of bells playing a tune. Once they have made sure all is well, they go back in again and the doors shut.

You can only really see the performance from the other side of the street. Mr Gruber says that goes to show you ought to look up from time to time as you are walking around London. Lots of people shuffle along staring at the pavement and miss things that way.

I still wonder how Mr Fortnum and Mr Mason persuaded a chicken to lay a Scotch egg in the first place. I expect the health and safety people would have something to say about it these days.

There are no prizes for guessing which shop has a revolving door that got jammed when I caught an expanding clothesline in it by mistake. It was a Christmas present for Mrs Bird and I shan't go shopping there again in a hurry. They might recognise me!

Last in line before you reach Green Park is the Ritz, and it's very grand. You need to book ahead to have tea (longer at weekends) and apart from the fact that the pot must be cold by then, you need to be properly dressed for the occasion, as I found out one day when they refused to let me in because I wasn't wearing a tie.

The other side of Piccadilly houses the Royal Academy of Arts, where the high spot each year is the Summer Exhibition of contemporary art. In between there are major exhibitions of collections on loan from all over the world.

Next door is the Burlington Arcade, which has a glass roof and shops on either side specialising in antique jewellery, cashmere jumpers, leather goods and other luxury items. Uniformed Beadles dressed in frock coats adorned with gold piping and wearing top

Royal Academy of Arts

Burlington Arcade

hats patrol the arcade to make sure there is no unseemly behaviour, like whistling or the shaking out of umbrellas after a rainstorm. You can even get your shoes cleaned while you are sitting down.

By then my own feet were beginning to feel as though they could do with a bit of a going over and I wouldn't have minded a rest, but unfortunately I wasn't wearing my wellington boots.

I expect we could have bought some very good buns at Fortnum & Mason, but we didn't have our deckchairs with us so we wouldn't have been able to sit on the pavement outside to enjoy them.

Besides, Mr Gruber said if we did that we would soon be arrested for causing a traffic jam. I didn't like to say it, but there seemed to be one already (another reason why the West End isn't ideal for small children, unless they are in pushchairs).

One way and another, Piccadilly has been the inspiration for lots of songs, books, films and plays over the years; even a comic opera.

But as we crossed back to the other side and I caught sight of some of the displays in Fortnum & Mason's windows I began to have other matters on my mind.

"That makes two of us," said Mr Gruber, when I told him my stomach was feeling a bit wibbly woo. "Sightseeing makes you peckish, Mr Brown. Follow me. I know just the place where we can get our second wind."

Without further ado he led the way back to Piccadilly Circus, turned right into the far side of the Haymarket, then left into Panton Street and on into Leicester Square.

Leicester Square is famous not only for its huge cinemas, but also for an old clockhouse that has been converted into a popular tourist information centre where you can purchase official theatre tickets at bargain prices.

Leicester Square

"Look at the clock. It's no wonder I was feeling hungry!"

old clockhouse

It is also full of restaurants, and I thought that might be where we were ending up. But Mr Gruber had other ideas. We carried on past the clockhouse, went down another short street and turned right into the Charing Cross Road, finishing up outside the National Portrait Gallery.

"It's right by Trafalgar Square and it has a restaurant on the top floor," explained Mr Gruber. "We can kill several birds with one stone: satisfy our appetites, plan out where we would like to go next and have a good rest at the same time."

He was certainly right about the first item on the agenda.

Never has a coconut bakewell pudding with vanilla custard and raspberry ripple ice cream, washed down with a cup of steaming hot cocoa, tasted so good.

Mr Gruber ordered the cheese plate with fruit-and-nut loaf, and we sat looking out of the window at the rooftops of London while we discussed our next outing.

"It *is* a lovely view," agreed a waitress, as she reeled off some of the sights that could be seen from the window: Big Ben, the London Eye, the Gherkin…

Mr Gruber added a few more ideas. Then he asked me what I would like to do on our next outing.

National Portrait Gallery

"Never mind the view. Taste the cocoa!"

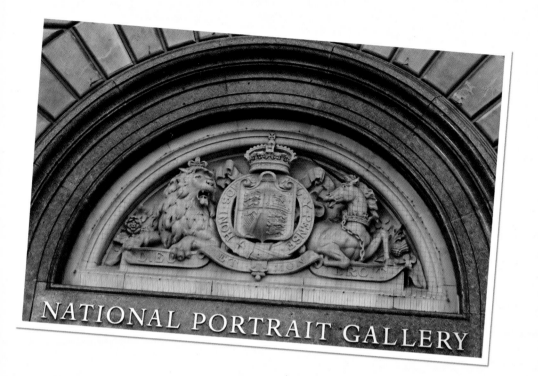

I was tempted by the Gherkin. Bears like anything new, and I had never been inside a gherkin before, but in the end something else the waitress said caught my fancy and it certainly turned out to be different from anything I had ever imagined.

But first I must tell you about the National Portrait Gallery, because if you want to know what people in history were like there is no better place.

A rotating selection of over 1,000 pictures of famous people is on display at any one time. The oldest is of King Henry VII, which was painted in 1505. Mr Gruber thinks he is looking cross because he wanted to marry the Emperor Maximilian's daughter and she had turned him down.

National Portrait Gallery

"I'm glad I don't have to dust them all"

The pictures are arranged in chronological order through the centuries until you reach the ground floor. When I went there was a motion picture of David Beckham fast asleep, which lasted an hour, so was really only a nap; and a painting of J. K. Rowling sitting in front of some boiled eggs. She seemed a bit glum too, and I didn't blame her. The eggs looked as though they had gone cold and she was probably wishing the artist would hurry up with his brushes.

Apart from all the paintings, the Gallery has a collection of over 220,000 photographs, and there is a large room by the main hall where you can view many of them on a bank of computer screens.

I chose a picture of Isambard Kingdom Brunel. He is standing in front of some huge launching chains belonging to a steamship called the *Great Eastern*, which he had designed. I expect it made a change from building railways. At the time it was the biggest in the world. I bought a postcard of the same picture for my Aunt Lucy on the way out. I expect she will put it on the notice board in the Home for Retired Bears.

I hadn't realised history could be so interesting, even though it took place a long time ago. As Mr Gruber says, it isn't simply a record of the people and the times in which they lived, it shows how painting and photography developed over the years.

The National Portrait Gallery is a lot less crowded than Madame Tussauds, so I can't wait to go back and visit the National Gallery next door as well.

National Portrait Gallery

"All good things come to an end"

TRAFALGAR SQUARE

Afterwards we walked round Trafalgar Square. Everything in the square is big – Nelson's Column is big, and so are the lions on either side of it. But somehow our visit to the gallery brought all the statues to life. Even Nelson on top of his pedestal, minus one arm and an eye, looked less stern than usual.

A small café is housed in the wall on the north side of the square and alongside the entrance to it there is a built-in replica of the official imperial standards of length: one inch, one foot, two feet and one yard. I must take my ruler along there one day and check it, in case I need to ask for my money back.

In a separate area to the south of the main square there is a statue of King Charles I mounted on a horse, looking very important. I suppose it is because by now he must realise he is the point from which all distances to London are measured.

Imperial standards of length

Every year on 21st October crowds gather to watch the Sea Cadet Corps hold a parade in honour of Nelson's victory at the Battle of Trafalgar. But the biggest crowds of all congregate around Christmas to greet the arrival from Oslo of a giant tree, given by Norway as a token of gratitude for Britain's support during World War II, and they reach their peak again on New Year's Eve.

Not *quite* everything in the square is big. Built into one of the lampposts in the southeast corner is the world's smallest police station. In the old days a policeman had to sit inside during less peaceful demonstrations and keep an eye on the crowds in case of trouble, so that he could put in a call for help if need be. But that doesn't happen any more. Modern means of communication have seen to that.

We found what we think may have been the lamppost in question, but when I looked through a glass panel in the door all I could see was a broom. Mr Gruber thought it would be nowhere big enough to sweep Trafalgar Square, so it's a bit of a mystery.

Old police station in lamppost

St Martin-in-the-fields

"Trust a bus to turn up when you don't want one!"

On the other side of the road to the east of Trafalgar Square stands the church of St Martin-in-the-Fields, which is also unique; not simply because when the original one was built in the twelfth century it was surrounded by fields, but for all the things that go on there today, such as free lunchtime concerts given by up-and-coming musicians.

But it is in the ancient vaults below ground that most of the activity takes place. The Café in the Crypt is huge and it's a good place to go for an inexpensive meal and there are sometimes live jazz concerts in the evening.

I thought that was where we were going next. But instead, we walked along the Strand and turned left into Bedford Street.

I nearly fell over backwards with surprise when all of a sudden I found myself in a different world. It's called Covent Garden and everywhere we looked there were musicians, clowns, tightrope walkers… there was even a man who looked as though he was made of silver. "I hope it doesn't rain," I said, as he bent down to shake my paw. "You might go rusty."

He didn't seem best pleased, so Mr Gruber felt for a coin.

"They are known as buskers," he explained. "It's how they earn their living. Lots of famous entertainers began that way."

covent Garden

Covent Garden

Then there was the Royal Opera House. We stood outside for a little while, listening to someone singing. When I tried joining in Mr Gruber suggested I might like to visit the London Transport Museum instead.

They have the real things there, not just models. I couldn't make up my mind whether I wanted to be a busker or a train driver. I don't suppose they have many bears driving trains on the Underground so there might be an opening.

Lift in the
pavement

I suppose all good things have to come to an end, otherwise you wouldn't have anything to look forward to, so I was glad Mr Gruber was with me, otherwise I would never have found my way back to St Martin-in-the-Fields. And I certainly wouldn't have looked for a modern lift in the pavement outside.

It takes you straight down to brass rubbing in the Crypt. Children are welcome and all the materials needed to do it themselves – such as waxy crayons and paper – are available for hire. There is a large display of replica brasses to practise on, but be warned – don't choose one of the knights; some of them are taller than me and they use up a lot of material.

In fact, by then it wasn't the brass I wanted to rub, it was my eyes. "I'm afraid my lids are getting very heavy, Mr Gruber," I called.

"In that case," said Mr Gruber, "I suggest we call it a day, Mr Brown. An early night would do us both good."

Brass rubbing in the Crypt

"I wish I hadn't chosen something quite so large!"

GALLERIES AND MUSEUMS

The next morning Mrs Bird said I slept like a log, but in fact I had been dreaming about galleries and museums.

London has so many of both there wouldn't be room to list them all, let alone visit them, so I have made a list of the ones I think are the most interesting.

To start with, on Lancaster Road, which is very near the Portobello Road, there is John Opie's Museum of Brands, Packaging and Advertising. Over the years Mr Opie has amassed an enormous collection of everyday items dating back to the nineteenth century: matchboxes, bottles, tins of this, that and the other, labels, magazines. There are so many different things they threaten to outdo the Portobello Road itself.

It bears out what Mr Gruber is always saying. Never throw anything away. If you keep it long enough, one day it will become an antique.

I don't think I would ever have visited the British Library, near St Pancras Station, had it not been for him saying more than once that I really should go. It's so vast, with over fourteen million books on its shelves, I would have been frightened to go in by myself in case I got lost, so Jonathan and Judy went with me.

But then King John wouldn't have signed the Magna Carta in Runnymede in 1215 had it not been for others insisting he did. He certainly couldn't have pictured that one day people would be able to read it simply at the touch of a finger on a screen, and turn the pages too. But that ancient document and many others, for instance the first Shakespeare Folio, are among over 200 available to view free of charge in the Sir John Ritblat Gallery.

Jonathan and Judy were most impressed too, especially as they were studying for their exams. There are also a number of very good snack bars where you can sit and discuss what you have just seen.

The other three museums on my list are grouped at the bottom of Exhibition Road in South Kensington and regularly figure in the list of the ten most visited attractions.

"...and both the Victoria and Albert Museum and the Natural History Museum look like cathedrals"

Victoria and Albert Museum

Dedicated to the decorative arts, the Victoria and Albert Museum – entrance on the Cromwell Road – houses an unrivalled collection of over four million objects from all over the world, contained in four separate sections: Asia; Europe; Material & Techniques; and Modern. As well as Tipu's Tiger, which will interest small children, there are free activities for families everyday.

The Natural History Museum is housed in a Victorian building also with an entrance on the Cromwell Road. The exhibits – all eighty million of them – are once again divided into zones; Blue, Green, Orange and Red. If anyone had asked me what a lepidopterist is, I would have said it was someone who collects leopards, but it turns out to be butterflies and moths. The Natural History Museum has a collection of over thirteen million specimens!

You would be hard put to miss the enormous blue whale in the Mammals Gallery of the Blue Zone, or the various dinosaurs – including an animatronic Tyrannosaurus rex, which is so realistic it never fails to draw the crowds. An eight-storey high model of a cocoon and the Wildlife Garden in the Orange Zone are other musts before you finally tear yourself away.

Natural
History Museum

Next door, the Science Museum is a home from home for button-pressers of all ages, so packed full of hands-on exhibits it is impossible to take it all in during one visit. You can also buy tickets for "Wonderlab" on the third floor. This is an interactive science gallery, which is full of exciting experiments and activities for children of all ages.

Not only are all three museums free, but they provide an extraordinary amount of food for thought. Walking out into the daylight brings you back down to earth again with a vengeance.

"I was glad Mr Gruber was with me, otherwise I wouldn't have known where to go!"

Question: what building occupies a five-acre site in one of the most expensive areas of London? When it first opened in 1849 it was a small shop with just two assistants, and over the years it has grown to such an extent it now employs over 5,000 staff. Its motto is, "All Things for All People, Everywhere".

The answer lies but a short bus ride away from "Museumland" – or, if the weather is nice, a pleasant stroll along the Brompton Road to Knightsbridge…

KNIGHTSBRIDGE

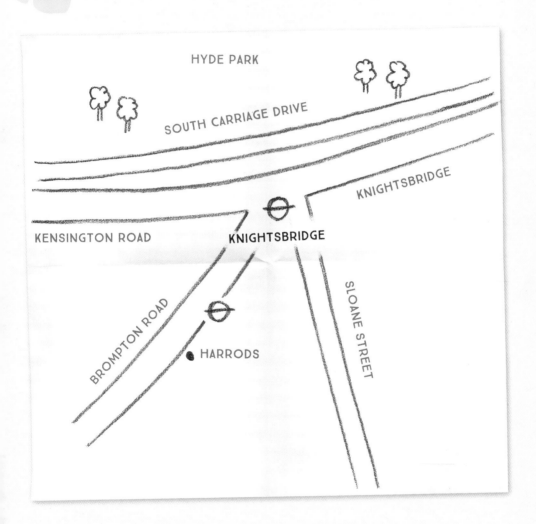

HYDE PARK

SOUTH CARRIAGE DRIVE

KNIGHTSBRIDGE

KENSINGTON ROAD

KNIGHTSBRIDGE

BROMPTON ROAD

SLOANE STREET

HARRODS

Once upon a time, along with nearby Chelsea, Knightsbridge was yet another example of a small village outside the City of London boundaries; a haunt of highwaymen lying in wait for people travelling westwards.

Now it is one of the most exclusive areas in London. Property values have soared out of all recognition and it is home to many famous names, the most famous one of all being Harrods.

It certainly lives up to its motto. People from all walks of life and all parts of the world flock there. On a good day over 300,000 pass through its doors, not necessarily to buy anything, but to gaze in awe at all the things there are on display, particularly in the food department, and that's what the man who started it, Charles Henry Harrod, was about, after all.

Harrods Food Hall

"Yums!"

I couldn't possibly leave Harrods empty-handed, so Mr Gruber bought me a donut. It was like a week's elevenses rolled into one.

Harrods Food Hall

WESTMINSTER

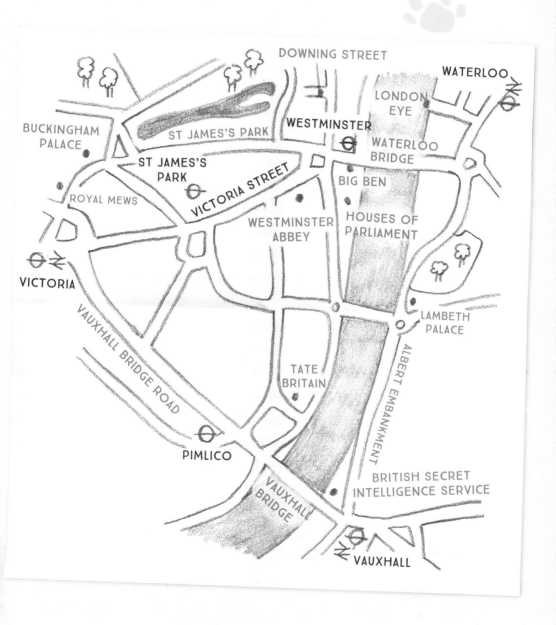

Horse Guards Parade

For our next outing, Mr Gruber suggested a tour of Westminster. We hailed a taxi from Westminster Underground, which took us past so many famous places – Big Ben, the Houses of Parliament, Horse Guards Parade – I had a job keeping up, but Mr Gruber explained everything.

A short while later we drove alongside the Queen's Gardens at Buckingham Palace but couldn't see in because there is a very high wall. I wish we had one like it. It would put paid to our bad-tempered neighbour, Mr Curry, looking into our garden. Perhaps the Queen has someone like him living next door.

Then we passed by the Royal Mews, which I had always thought was a cats' home, but it turned out to be where the Queen's horses and carriages are kept.

When we got out of the taxi at Buckingham Palace, Mr Gruber had a surprise for me. We were going to see the "Changing of the

Guard", which had been at the top of my list of things to do, and I must say I wasn't disappointed.

Weather permitting it takes place at 11.30 a.m. every day of the week during the summer months and every other day during winter, and it's free, so it's very good value. The best place to watch it from is the railings outside the Palace itself, but you need to get there early. Mind you, the ones on duty are so good I can't see why they need to be changed. It was exciting to watch them and one of the best days out I have been on.

Big Ben

"from a distance they reminded me of the jars of marmalade in Fortnum & Mason"

TOWER OF
LONDON

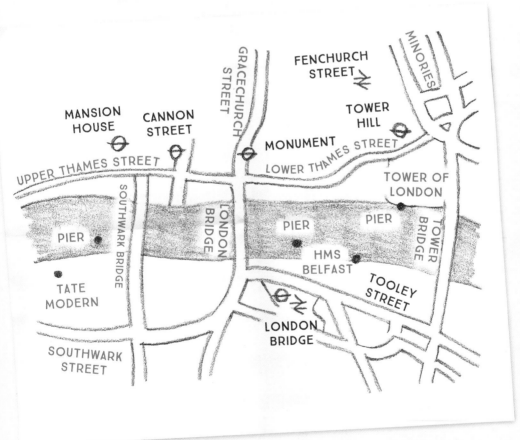

Mr Gruber is good at thinking up surprises. One day, when Jonathan and Judy were home from school, we caught a bus at Paddington Station. As it arrived he pointed up at something in the sky so we didn't see the destination board, and the journey seemed to go on for ever. Anyway, we suddenly turned a corner and found ourselves outside the Tower of London.

I won't tell you what happened that day, because some of you may have already read my book about it, but there are things you wouldn't find anywhere else in the world.

According to Mr Gruber, in recent years a miraculous transformation of signposting, shops and places to eat has quietly taken place; so much so that even the 1,000-year-old walls seem friendlier than they once were, which seems to have affected all those working there as well, except the ravens. It's hard to tell with ravens.

Tower Bridge

Tower of London

"It makes number 32 Windsor Gardens look very small"

HMS Belfast

Where else would you have genuine Beefeaters at your disposal to show you around and tell you all about the grisly events that took place there in the past? It should be a must on everyone's itinerary.

While you are in that part of London it would be a shame not to visit some of the other famous sites. For example, there is Tower Bridge with its wonderful view of the city from the overhead walkway.

And no small boy should be deprived of a visit to HMS *Belfast*, a cruiser moored on the other side of the river, which was commissioned in August 1939 and armed with twelve six-inch heavy guns. Mr Gruber says the story of the last surviving example of a big cruiser's time at sea in many theatres of war and the battles she fought before finally being turned into a museum is a stirring tribute to all who sailed in her. Sensible (i.e. flat) shoes should be worn and it is suggested that one and a half to two hours should be allowed.

My tip for the day: after our visit to the tower, we caught a high-speed Thames Clipper at the Tower Pier. We took one to the Embankment and the Underground station for home.

The boats are called catamarans and they are very wide, so it's best to get a seat in the front row if you can so that you have a clear view out of both sides.

"There is something exciting happening every which way you look!"

The first stop is at London Bridge City Pier where you have a good view of the new bridge. The old one was bought by an American millionaire who had it shipped over to the States and re-erected in the Nevada Desert.

London Bridge

The second stop is at Bankside, alongside a replica of Shakespeare's Globe theatre, and ahead of it is a vast building that once upon a time provided the electricity for London, but is now one of the largest and busiest museums in the world: the Tate Modern.

The ground floor alone, where the giant generators used to stand, is so breathtakingly large that visitors of all ages can only gaze in wonder when they see it for the first time. Now home to a series of equally spectacular travelling exhibits, the rest of the building houses all that's best in modern art.

After leaving Bankside the boat crosses to the other side of the river, stopping first at Blackfriars and then Embankment where we were disembarking. But shortly before that happened Mr Gruber told me to watch out for the 1,500-year-old Cleopatra's Needle. It's twenty-one metres high, so it's hard to miss.

It had been a lovely day and part of me wanted it to go on for ever.

Tate Modern

"It's another gallery that doesn't look like one"

REGENT'S CANAL AND REGENT'S PARK

SWISS COTTAGE

ADELAIDE ROAD

CHALK FARM

CAMDEN LOCK

MARKET

PRIMROSE HILL

AVENUE ROAD

CAMDEN TOWN

ABBEY ROAD

WELLINGTON ROAD

ST JOHN'S WOOD

LONDON ZOO

ALBANY ROAD

REGENT'S PARK

LISSON GROVE

WARWICK AVENUE

EDGWARE ROAD

GREAT PORTLAND STREET

MARYLEBONE

LITTLE VENICE

EDGWARE ROAD

BAKER STREET

REGENT'S PARK

I think Mr Gruber must have been feeling much the same way because one morning soon afterwards he asked me if I would care to join him in an outing on the Regent's Canal.

I jumped at the idea, so we set off for Browning's Pool in Little Venice – so called because a famous poet called Mr Browning lived there – which is where a lot of boats are moored.

It was lucky I woke up earlier than usual that morning because we were just in time to catch the 10.30 a.m. narrowboat as it was about to leave its moorings opposite number 42 Blomfield Road.

The boat is called *Jason* and it's Mr Gruber's favourite because it is an authentic twenty-two-metre narrowboat that began its working life over one hundred years ago, carrying coal and other heavy freight. In 1951 it underwent conversion and took on a new lease of life when it was licensed to take passengers on pleasure trips between Little Venice and Camden Lock, a couple of miles or so away.

Jason

Little Venice →

On the way out there is a live commentary so you learn a lot of interesting things about the history of canals and the places you are passing on the way.

It is so peaceful travelling along at a maximum speed of four miles an hour it's hard to believe you are still in London. (Mind you, that's a lot faster than the traffic in Piccadilly the day I was there!)

The Thames is exciting because there is always something going on, but the special thing about being on a canal is that for most of the time you travel behind places, so you enter a whole new world you wouldn't normally see. People are much friendlier too. They even wave as you go past, which is most unusual in London.

At one point we found ourselves passing through the back of London Zoo. There were warthogs to be seen on one side of the boat and tropical birds in the vast aviary on the other.

Soon after I went to live with the Browns, Jonathan and Judy took me to London Zoo. They thought it would be a treat. I didn't say so at the time, but I was worried I might not be allowed out again. I didn't like the way most of the animals were behind bars, and it left me feeling rather sad.

But when I saw the warthogs I felt things might be different – they seemed free to come and go as they pleased and they hardly gave us a second glance.

I was just beginning to wish I could do all my travelling by canal boat in future, when we drew near a very strange-looking craft. It was painted red and it had two storeys, rather like a house.

But before I had a chance to ask what it was we took a sharp turn to the left, and headed for Camden Lock, where those passengers who had a one-way ticket could disembark and explore the market.

Camden Lock →

camden Market ⟶

Mr Gruber had never been there before either, so for once we were doing something new together, which made it extra special.

"That boat you saw, Mr Brown," he said, "was a well-known floating Chinese restaurant called Feng Shang Princess. It's a welcoming hint of what to expect – Camden is a very cosmopolitan part of London to say the least."

I looked around and sure enough we were surrounded by stalls selling food from all manner of different countries: Turkey, Morocco, Thailand, Vietnam, Brazil, Italy…

I think Mr Gruber was as surprised as I was; and as we penetrated further and further inside the market itself, so it became more and more like an Aladdin's Cave and more and more crowded, and noisier!

It was *so* busy that I held on to my hat in case it got knocked off my head.

"It's a good job we came on a weekday, Mr Brown," he gasped. "They do say over 100,000 people visit here on a Sunday."

The hustle and bustle was making me feel quite hungry so Mr Gruber suggested we go back to the food stalls. It didn't take us long to find one with delicious-looking Italian dishes. Italians are famous for three things: ice cream, home-made pasta and making everyone feel welcome – especially, as it turned out, bears. Mr Gruber ordered a Fiorentina pizza for me and a home-made lasagne for himself.

When my pizza arrived it was so big that passers-by gathered round to have a look. Mr Gruber wanted to take a photograph of it, but he had left his wide-angle lens behind, so I ate as much as I could and then asked the people at the stall for a box to take the rest home.

Mr Gruber insisted I have an ice cream on our way back and I didn't want to let him down, so I had a strawberry water ice in a cone.

Mrs Bird was worried because I didn't want any supper that night. She thought I was sickening for something.

Before I went to sleep I wrote a postcard to my Aunt Lucy. I wanted to tell her all about my day out, but there was only room to say it ended up with one of the best meals I'd had in a long time. Luckily there were so many pizza stains on the card by the time I finished it looked good enough to eat, so I expect she put two and two together.

"My ice cream cone soon became history!"

One thing leads to another, so it wasn't surprising that after my brief glimpse of London Zoo that was where Mr Gruber and I went next. Sure enough, so many changes had taken place I hardly recognised it.

Where there were once bars, there is now glass, and all the inhabitants live in spacious enclosures as near as it is possible to be to their natural habitats.

Pride of place goes to the Gorilla Kingdom; a huge moated island planted out to replicate a forest clearing in Central Africa, complete with the kind of flora they like to eat.

There is a high-level viewing platform, which enables visitors to meet giraffes face to face, and a walk-through Bird Safari incorporating trees and a bridge over a stream. While you are there, watch out for the clock outside the Blackburn Pavilion as it strikes the half hour. It will make you laugh.

Today's London Zoo is all about research into the preservation and continuation of animal life on planet Earth. It receives no state funding, and raises money wherever it can.

"I think the lion had his eye on my sandwiches, but Mr Gruber said you aren't supposed to feed the animals, so I quickly hid them"

London Zoo

"'What's under your hat?'
asked the giraffe"

To that end, for four days in 2005 they put eight humans on display in the old Mappin Terraces. I wish I had known. I would have taken them sandwiches filled with Mrs Bird's home-made marmalade. That would have kept them from becoming extinct!

Over the years there are two things I have learned about Mr Gruber. One is that he is very fond of surprises, and secondly he likes saving the best until last. The best in this case turned out to be Regent's Park.

Regent's Park owes its existence to the fact that in 1817 the Prince Regent commissioned a famous architect, Mr Nash, to build him a summer residence on what had been yet another royal hunting ground. The grandiose plan included among other things the construction of fifty-six villas inside the park for friends of the Court; terraces round the perimeter; and what amounted to an unobstructed view of Carlton House near the seat of power in Westminster, which is how Regent Street came to be built.

In the years that followed, the prince became so taken up with overseeing work on Buckingham Palace prior to his enthronement as King George IV that work was eventually abandoned. Only three of the eight completed villas survive to this day, but fortunately for us, not only Regent Street, but also the Nash-inspired terraces were all completed and now provide a wonderful background to much of the park.

Regent's Park

There is a lot of food for thought in Regent's Park

Regent's Park is special because its 400 or so acres are part play area, part nature reserve; the winding paths criss-crossing it reveal surprises at every turn, and cater for all tastes.

There are playing fields for football, cricket and Sunday morning baseball; Queen Mary's Gardens and the wonderful Rose Gardens in particular; an outdoor theatre seating 1,200 during the summer months, staging up to four different productions each year (rendered even more magical as night falls on a summer's evening); regular concerts in the bandstand; boating on the main lake and a smaller lake with pedalos especially for children next to an adventure playground.

And everywhere there is an award-winning restaurant not far away where you can sit and absorb it all at your leisure.

But as Mr Gruber says, these things don't just happen. As with London Zoo, a great deal of work goes on behind the scenes.

Despite being in the heart of London, Regent's Park is home to at least 200 species of birds, including such rarities as the peregrine falcon. There are mammals galore, and more than 650 waterfowl on the boating lake, along with carp, gudgeon, roach and

"wonderfully aloof from it all"

sticklebacks, the latter kept safe from predatory herons breeding on the islands by the planting of reed beds and other forms of refuge.

With nearly one hundred different species of swans, geese and ducks to care for, striking a happy balance in catering for their different needs can be no easy task.

To their very great credit they must have got it right because it is now the centre for breeding waterfowl for all the other Royal Parks in London, and during the spring and autumn, migrating birds, both going and coming back, use the park as a safe stopping-off place for refreshment.

THE LONDON EYE

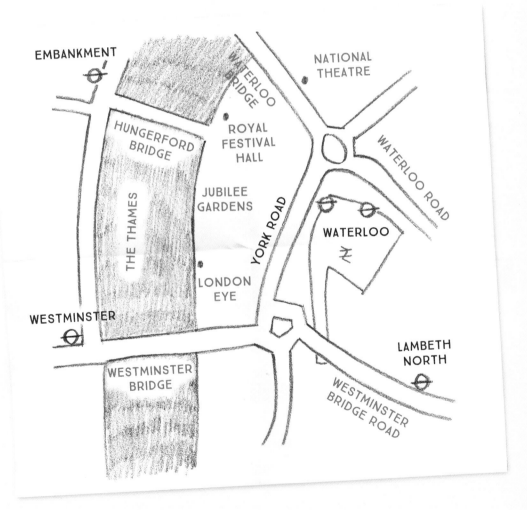

It wasn't so long ago that I first went on the London Eye. My long lost Uncle Pastuzo arrived out of the blue one day, and while he was passing through he treated all the family, along with Mr Gruber and me, to a flight.

So I was rather surprised when, thanks to Mr Gruber, I found myself on it again. Not that I'm grumbling, of course. I was so excited the first time I didn't make the most of the occasion. Also, I wasn't too sure I liked the term "flight"; it made it sound as if our capsule might become detached on the way round, but we all came back in one piece.

It was like a dream: there one moment – gone the next. Although I have since learned that as it only travels at roughly twice the speed of an average tortoise it takes about thirty minutes to complete each revolution.

As you may have noticed, Mr Gruber has been responsible for overseeing some of the entries in this book. For one thing, he is much better at spelling than I am. Take Kew Gardens. I spent days looking for it under the letter "Q", so we never did get there!

It's still on the list of places I would like to visit one day, along with Hampstead Heath, the City of London, the Shard and the London Wetland Centre.

As our capsule reached its highest point I looked out at the slowly passing scene. London seemed vast from 130 metres in the air. There was nothing but buildings stretching as far as the horizon in all directions. For all I knew there might be other villages awaiting their turn to be swallowed up.

"I hope we don't become detached, Mr Gruber"

"London looks so big from up here, don't suppose I sha ever see it all"

West

I had never felt so small. Now, even the Houses of Parliament seemed like a model.

"I don't suppose I shall ever see everything there is to be seen, Mr Gruber," I said.

"I doubt if anyone has done that, or ever will," said Mr Gruber. "If Doctor Johnson were alive today, he might say: 'He who claims he has seen everything there is to see in London must either be very tired or he is telling fibs.'

"People often start by thinking they know it all, but the more you learn, the more you realise how little you really know. It can be very humbling.

"Which is why I brought you on this trip. Being a bear with an enquiring mind has stood you in good stead. It's rewarding that you are able to share your experiences with others. I trust we shall have many more outings together."

As we began our downward flight he reached in his pocket and took out a small leatherbound notebook. It had my initials, P. B., on the front.

"I know you will make good use of it for your jottings, Mr Brown," he said, waving aside my thanks.

But that's Mr Gruber all over. As I said at the beginning, he is my best friend, and it's nice having things you can look forward to.

TRAVEL INFORMATION

GETTING AROUND

Because London is so big, the best way to see it is sitting down. City pavements are bad enough if you only have paws, but they can be very tiring for small feet too.

TAXIS

London taxi drivers are the best in the world. Mr Gruber says that's because they have to spend anything up to four years braving the elements on two wheels in order to learn all the street names before they are allowed anywhere near a taxi. They are wonderfully adept at picking their way through traffic but be warned, if you hire one for the day you should arrange a government loan first. The drivers are a mine of information, but either they talk all the time or they don't say a word. It would be very unlucky if you got one who didn't talk!

UNDERGROUND TRAINS

The Underground trains are fast and efficient. Maps are free and the different lines are colour-coded. The downside is that you miss what's going on above ground. All you have to look at are the advertisements and people eating their sandwiches.

BUSES

There is a huge network of bus routes, but until you get to know London it's hard to know which one to take.

BIG BUS TOURS

If you are only in London for a short stay, the best way of getting your bearings is by a "hop-on, hop-off", open-topped bus. The ticket lasts for two days and buses call at most of the main sights, but if you see something interesting on the way you can hop off at the nearest stop en route, and hop on the next bus when you have seen what you want to see.

My Tip: I think the open top deck is best, but on cold days take plenty of warm clothing, and during the summer wear a hat to avoid sunstroke. The first time I went on one I hopped on and hopped off on one leg by mistake. The rest of the passengers followed suit.

The driver could hardly believe his eyes.

INDEX

ACKNOWLEDGEMENTS

Paddington and the publishers thank the following for their kind co-operation with the photography involved in this book; Burlington Arcade, Daunt Books, Fortnum & Mason, Hamleys, Harrods, London Eye, National Portrait Gallery, the Orangery, Paul Rothe & Son, St Martin-in-the-Fields.

Every effort has been made to trace the copyright holders of the material in this book and to ensure the accuracy of the factual information included. If any rights have been omitted, or any factual errors have occurred, the publishers offer to rectify in a future edition, following notification.